I've Loved You Since Forever

I've Loved You Since Forever

Hoda Kotb

pictures by Suzie Mason

HARPER

An Imprint of HarperCollinsPublishers

ISBN 978-0-06-284174-2 (trade bdg.)

ISBN 978-0-06-285170-3 (special edition)

The artist used Adobe Photoshop to create the digital illustrations for this book.

Typography by Chelsea C. Donaldson

18 19 20 21 22 PC 10 9 8 7 6 5 4 3 2 1

❖

First Edition

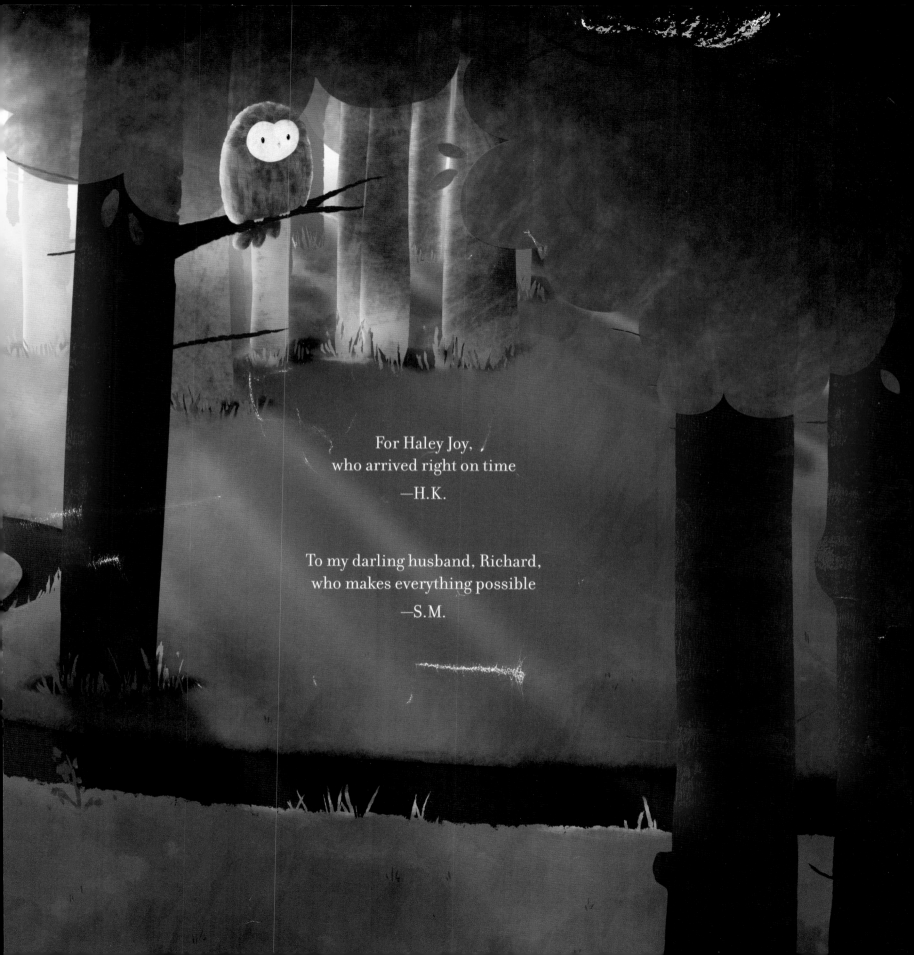

For Haley Joy,
who arrived right on time
—H.K.

To my darling husband, Richard,
who makes everything possible
—S.M.

I've loved you since forever.

Before birds flew over rainbows

and monkeys swung on trees,

there was you...

and there was me.

Before the sun rose in the sky

and honey came from bees,

there was you...

and there was me.

I've loved you since forever.

Before the moon lit up the night

and elephants wandered free,

there was you....

and there was me.

Before otters swam together

and rivers reached the sea,

there was you

and there was me,

waiting for the day our stars would cross

and you and I turned into we.